ART TRAP

REMYA RAJKUMAR

ISBN 979-888569679-1

Contents

CHAPTER ONE

Chapter One

As I sit by the window, on a moonlit rainy night, all I could hear is music played by the sky, sometimes it feels as if it's a rock song, and sometimes it feels like its sad hymn. I look towards my bed, I see nothing but loneliness. It is a huge bed, having lots of pillows, and yet I sit by the window side, hoping my cage will soon be open. I wonder why it that we are caged is. Why our wings are always tied? Why don't we live life the way we want? I think about all these, but all I could is think, I can never speak, for even if I were to speak I wouldn't be heard. In a way I am grateful that I would never be able to speak for I was born special as people call it. My room is actually more special than me, I don't know what would have happened to me if it weren't for the books which never failed to give me company. I am in my second year of college, and so far I have made no friends or so called gang. I was just in some other world all the time. I would spend all my time in library without getting a bit bored. That's the power of stories; they can transform you into some magical world. It is from the habit of reading, I developed the habit of drawing. My imagination was quite good, I guess, which helped me to draw. I am an artist, I had the ability to create magic with my paint brush, at least that's what everyone told me, I never believed in magic.

Maybe it's because I never experienced magic.

My inability to speak is highly connected to my inability to express myself. I never felt the need either, I was so in my world that I never felt connected to outside world. I had huge collection of books, sometimes I read the same ones again and again, and every time I read I got some new opinions. I never had a real friend, apart from my family I avoided humans, not that I hate but I kind of didn't like, the reason is simple. I always got the same reactions from people, either sympathy or being checked upon every time to see if I am okay , or those who try to take benefit of me, for the simple reason that I am a woman. I really pitied them, it is nice to be like this, even if I talk, no one would know. I didn't know though what my dream or my purpose in life is, I guess no one really knows Normally, people like me, who have some sort of special condition or in normal term disability, God gifts them with some other thing, maybe music, maybe cooking skills, it could be anything, I wondered what is mine but I never got any answer. Sometimes in life though we feel like we are in the end of our life, we feel as if we are simply walking without any destination. So many people say the journey is better than destination but what if there is no journey itself. I have always been amused by the word love. It's just a small four letter word though the way in which it is used and felt is infinite yet we try to control it in this four letter word.

Love, this one word which embraces everything is what was missing in my life. I was loved, by everyone I knew, but I never felt it, maybe because I wasn't able to express it properly. The sky seemed beautiful at night. It felt as it was waiting to be heard. It is just wonderful how the moon looked at night sky. I look towards my empty canvas, waiting to be drawn. My brush seemed to want my embrace, but I didn't know what is it that I should draw, for my imagination was numb. I look up at the sky again, stars shining brightly, raindrops kissing the ground, the sweet melody of sky. I had lit my night lamp, took my notebook and pen, and went to my chair. I sat in silence for some time. It is strange how mind works, I was thinking something else and I reached somewhere else. It is not the first time that I saw this person when I closed my eyes. He was huge, like princes of old times. He was standing there and smiling at me, lending me his hand. I wasn't sure if it was me on the other end, but somewhere looked like me, I had just become huge I guess. I could feel him coming near, my breathes suddenly started to increase, I wanted to open my eyes but I wasn't able to, it took few minutes to force my eyes to open. It has been like that always whenever I thought of love this person's face would come up. I notice there is a pen lying between paint brushes, I hasn't used it till now. I take that pen, open the cap. It had beautiful nib. I hold it amongst my fingers; I could feel a shiver passing by my whole body. I take my notebook, turning the pages. Tonight I didn't feel like drawing. I look at the sky again, smiled at the moon, and closed my eyes taking a sigh. I just got a wonderful flow of thoughts which just came to me randomly. Without much thinking, I start writing something like,

Come, let's go...Somewhere far...Where nothing ties us,
Where we are free to fly, in a world of our own
Where there will be no one else, where we could stop time...
Moon is winking at me...Asking me why do I think so much?
I don't think of the sun....Though we never meet....
For I know we belong to the same sky...love...

I need to shine now then only my sun would come bright in the morning....

He dies every night just for me to shine...And I die every morning for him to shine...

So strange our love is...Even though we are separated...

We are in love so much that time stands still in front of us...

Let time separate us and let anything come by our way...

Our love and shall stand strong....

I smile at the moon...wondering her pain...

I think of you...and all I wish is ...come let us also be under the sky called love...

For everything in this earth and above is love...just close your eyes and feel the sky above...

We can see the love of sun and moon. Who died every day for each other...?

And maybe like that one day you might see me too...Waiting...

To fly...to be somewhere far...

Away from the noise of the world...where there is just the two of us...free in love...always...where time stands still...

Waiting for us....

I have no idea as to when I had slept off. I heard my sister, she was calling my name. She was asking me to wake up as it was time for class. I make weird face on her, she understands I don't have mood to go today. She smiles and asks what lectures I had today. I show her the time table. She pats my shoulder and shows me that it's okay. She wasn't like me, she had lots of friends. For me my only friend in college was books again. Communicating was hard, I believe even if I had the ability to speak I wouldn't be able to make friends like her, she is a lovely person. One of the person I love the most, my only best friend. After she leaves, I look at my notebook. It was laying there open, pages were moving along with the wind. I leave it as it is; I wanted to sleep little more time properly. I drag myself towards bed. Recent times I have been seeing this person a lot in my dreams. I wanted to find out who it was, but didn't feel that curious either.

I woke up after a while, and went towards my mother; she just smiled and said, "Today also you didn't go?"

I just smile back and nod. I rush to my room again. I couldn't be outside my room for more than fifteen minutes. It was like some sort of escape room for me. Only my parents and sister could come anytime, anyone else is not at all allowed. Even them, they aren't allowed to enter my inner room, which was actually my painting room. They saw most of my works but not all. I rush to my room, I take my sketch book. I could feel my fingers had to draw something different today. After a while, I realized that it was the same person I had seen in my dreams that I was drawing now. He did look good. He was sitting on horse, with a sword. Behind him, I had drawn traces of a palace. It was stone built one, surrounded with huge trees, and mountains. It took few hours to complete but it was worth the time. I check my mobile, I had received message from Jai my only other friend who could understand me a little I could say. He wanted to meet me, I don't know why, but I say okay as it has been long time since I met him, he was my school friend. He messaged me again in a while that he would come over to my house to meet me, I felt relieved, and I don't have to go out today. Time went quite fast. It was evening when he came; he came to my room slowly calling my name. I went to open the door, he runs inside pushing me aside, and ask me to sit down. He too talks a lot like my sister. I listen to all of his stories, I liked his company even if he talked a lot, and it didn't bore me like others maybe because he thought of me as a friend. His eyes falls on the sketch which I drew, I had colored it half. He says its beautiful and all I just nod. He leaves after that, I look at it again closely, wondering who this might be who always comes in my dreams. I opened my textbooks, checked what is there tomorrow. I couldn't bunk every day and hence I forced myself to sleep. I didn't know 24 hours would go so fast.

The next morning, as I open my eyes, I see my notebook open, and there were words on it, I clearly remember I hadn't written anything, it was written:

Let us choose one another as companions!
Let us sit at each other's feet!
Inwardly we have many harmonies—think not
That we are only what we see.

No matter who we are or where we live, deep inside we all feel incomplete. It's like we have lost something and need to get it back. Just what that something is, most of us never find out. And of those who do, even fewer manage to go out and look for it.

Choose Love, Love! Without the sweet life of love,
Living is a burden—as you have seen.
Love is the water of life

May love find you when you least expect, where you least expect.

It was the best handwriting I had ever seen till date, I knew it was Rumi's words. I had no idea though as to who had written it. I thought of all possibilities yet nothing was convincing enough. I gave up thinking, just decided to leave, it might be just a dream. The next night, it was raining again, I sat in the chair, I opened the pens cap, and held it between my fingers, oh, what beautiful feel it was, suddenly I opened the notebook and my hand started to move on its own. The pen drove my hand, and started to speak. I was still in confusion of what was happening.

First it went on to write, “Hi, Hope you have liked my surprise, am impressed with your artistic skills, but I wonder, why so you have so much pain? What is the pain which you are always talking about?” I didn’t know if I was supposed to write or not but I decided to give it a try so I wrote, “Hello, I don’t really know if its surprise, it’s more of shock. I am sorry but I don’t think I need to share it now, and am quite surprised as well, that you can write by yourself? Are you some magic pen or something?”

There was a gap then again, my fingers just went that’s all I know and wrote, “Okay, tell me when you want to, well, what did you think, there are words dying inside me as well, just like you, I wish to be heard too, only if someone is there to listen, for I too don’t have voice, only words and most of the time silence. Silence is my voice as well.”

I felt bad so I wrote, “I am there for you too, and you can share your pain when you feel like.”

The conversation went on. We became friends quite fast and unexpectedly. Pen would advise me what I should draw when I was confused, what I should react even what I should be thinking about some topics. It was an interesting relation which no one could understand. In some days we became best friends, I forgot every other thing in world, it was only my new best friend which mattered to me, I took the notebook and pen wherever I went, and we were never away. I admired the opinions, ideas, time just seemed awesome. When you are weird everyone notices it and my family had noticed my changes, they were just concerned, and I don’t blame them , for they have tolerated me and my tantrums a lot, always forgiven me, so I didn’t mind it. They were the only humans I liked and loved and adored in this whole world.

One night, while I was asleep, something woke me up I rushed towards the notebook, searching everywhere for pen, it was nowhere to be found, I felt sad, I started crying. I never knew tears could fall like that from my eyes. It started flowing, I could feel heaviness, it didn't want to stop, I blamed myself, cursed myself for losing my only best friend, I didn't know what to do.

I held notebook close by my chest with the page open in which it was written, "I will be back soon...wait for me... my beautiful princess." I wiped my tears. I was smiling and blushing, but then in a moment I was crying again, what if it was lie? What if someone had stolen it? I should tell someone but whom? No one would really know which amongst them got lost and I don't know how to explain either, I decided to wait. It was weird and foolish but I didn't feel like anything else. I was disturbed, irritated, frustrated; all I could think have was about my precious pen. After some days, it was raining heavily, I had put on lamp, but it went off, power cuts, it was late night or in the early hours of morning, so no one would really know if power went off to switch on the generator. I went by the window side, sat there, it was thundering and lightning, rain was pouring down heavily and it felt as if sky was in pain too, as if it were shedding tears off. I just sat there in silence, for I didn't feel like doing anything else at that time.

CHAPTER TWO

Days went by, nothing happened, I had lost my interest in everything, I didn't read, I didn't write, I didn't eat, I didn't sleep, I was just on bed. I had even stopped drawing. I felt quite frustrated all the time. I didn't even come out of my room, doctors came to check, and I was perfectly healthy, nothing wrong. It is nothing but a proof that body and mind are different, and at times body doesn't react to the changes in mind. The communication between me and my family had always been through sign language. It seemed more like dance to me, I preferred to write but then it wasn't possible all the time. I was used to it, the sympathy, the taunts, the words which I wish I could have said if only I had voice. I am selfish person I guess, for I was concerned only about my wishes, my pain, my sorrow, my possessions and nothing else. I don't know if it's right or wrong, but that is what I am. I woke up every day with the hope, hope another mysterious word, which makes or in a way fools us to be something else. My faith didn't go less; I spent hours staring to those words. Finally, I dismissed such thoughts, I realized it's baseless, not going to classes, it was just my imagination, so I woke up finally from a long dream. I got back to my life, made myself busy. It was like I was going through a break up, but I couldn't say this to anyone because no one would understand it.

In between seeing me in such sorrow, my sister had advised Jai to come over and talk to me. My mother came along with him in my room to tell me that he was here. He came and sat next to me, he said, “So what is going on mystery girl, what is happening, why you haven’t replied to any of my messages?”

I just look at him, wondering if I should share with him what had happened. I decide to give it a try. He tells me the latest news happening in the campus. I knew it would be the same rubbish happening in our campus. I take my notebook and he says, “Maya there is nothing to be written down, what is this?” I show him, I ask him to read it. He reads all the conversations and I could see his face change.

He asks me, “What are you doing to yourself; you are talking to yourself in another handwriting?” I tell him that it is the pen, he asks me where it was, and I couldn’t find it. I show him few of my drawings which I had drawn as per his instruction.

Jai was getting irritated; he asked me “Is this some kind of new joke? This isn’t funny. And in case you are serious, this is foolishness; I can’t believe you fell for a pen?” I got furious hearing this; I didn’t fall for a pen. I could see he was having teary eyes, I ask what happened. He just says nothing, and after a while he confesses that he likes me. I felt happy, because I know I will be happy with him. I smile with bit of blushing; I guess he understood my answer. He was also smiling. It was time for him to leave; he gave me kiss suddenly and ran out of my room. He turned back while going and I was smiling. It felt like that perfect movie scene.

I was back to my normal life, when again one night, it was raining heavily, I loved to look at the sky when it rained. I was feeling so happy, as my life had new beginning. It was foolish to believe a pen and all but what happened after that was nice. I have a best friend now and he is also my partner in everything. I opened the windows, closed my eyes and went forward, raindrops kissed my cheeks. I went more forward, feeling each rain drop on my skin. I started playing with them, as each drop passed, trying to catch them and then letting it go. I was enjoying rain, after all this time; it is now that I really felt the beauty of rain. I closed the windows, and as I turned back I saw someone standing there, I was scared to death. With the kind of things happening in our society I could think of everything that could happen and no one would ever know if I was alive or dead for the ones with voice are not able to escape what would I do.

I moved back trying to get hold of sharp object, the stranger was looking straight to my eyes, observing me , and smiling , I couldn't clearly get what his intentions were , he seemed nice. I moved back and he took a step forward. He came towards the chair, looked at notebook which was lying in the floor. He took the notebook in his hands, and looked at me again smiling. I was confused more than scared, what he wants. I hated when someone invaded my privacy. I liked being alone, playing with words, or drawing up things I imagined. I didn't like social media. I didn't feel it like media at all, take any social media platform all you could see is, there pictures, it's as if there is no moment in their life which goes without posting update. People would comment, wow, nice, you look good, and stuff like that, no one would ever even say hi if you met in real. Everyone is online but do they even talk. I felt it way to out of my league, and stayed away besides, my only friends are my family and these books and pens, that are my world. It is so strange; all these thoughts were passing by me when I am confronted with a total stranger. I take look closer that's when I realise he has the face of the person I drew. I was feeling really nervous now; did I just bring a sketch to life?

He was still looking at me, smiling, finally he broke silence, he sat in stool which was there, and said, "Have a seat please." I moved the chair bit and sat. Just as much as I hated humans, I hated human touch also. I hated it when anyone touches me, it might be weird but I didn't like it at all. He spoke again, "You didn't recognize me didn't you?" He was smiling again looking at me , I tried to remember all guys whom I have known, I haven't known much because I didn't like them. I gave an expression of me –don't-know-who-the-hell-you-are-please-fuck-off.

He seemed to get it, he spoke again "When I wasn't here you were crying and all, now when I am back you don't recognise me, you even drew me."

I felt like hitting him, I didn't even look at him this time, he continued, "I told you I will be back my princess."

I looked up, my eyes opened wide, I didn't believe it yet, because it could be someone who has read it and fooling me, so I waited to hear what he was saying.

He continued, "I know you don't believe me, but..." He fell silent, and after few moments, he spoke exactly what we had spoken before, I wasn't yet convinced. I thought it was Jai, only he knew about this, but he wouldn't memorize these to fool me. He took notebook, kept it aside; he spoke about me, things which I hadn't shared to anyone than to those papers. I was convinced now but how did that pen become a human , that was what kept running in my mind, I wanted to ask but how would I ask, it's in times like this that I hated myself.

He somewhat understood I guess, he said, "I know what you are thinking, how did I become I human isn't it? Human mind has the power to do anything, you don't belong in here that is why when time came, you had drawn your home, and I, for you belong to me."

I shrugged; I knew it was a lie. What is this, firstly how dare he come to my room? I went to my parent's room; I woke them up, made them come to my room. I told them in actions that there is someone. They searched everywhere, they couldn't see anyone. My mother woke my sister by then. She told my sister to sleep with me. I felt relieved.

I went to my sister's room. It was exact opposite of mine. Her room was how a girl would keep it. All pinkish and girlish. Whatever it was, she was one of my closest friends. She could understand whatever I had in my mind.

She asked me, "Maya, what happened, saw any dream or read any book?" I didn't say anything. She said again, "Okay, don't worry, if you want to share, am here okay?" She smiled, I smiled back I did want to share, but how would I share? I messaged Jai too, he just replied saying that I might have dreamt nothing else. I went and took a sketchbook. I told her to wait, she said she will, but by the time I finished drawing, she had slept. We studied in the same college. She was a year elder to me.

The next day while going she said, "I read what you wrote, is it true? I mean all these happen? I have only seen in movies." I shrugged again. She asked if someone was doing this purposely and if I had told this to Jai, I nodded. We both left to our classes. The day went as usual, it was fine, and though I was scared nothing happened. We returned back, I said I would sleep with her tonight also. She said I should sleep in my room, and if something like that happens, she would come out, she would hide somewhere. I waited eagerly for him to come. He came, as expected, in some weird type of dress.

He was smiling, and said, “You don’t believe me don’t you? That’s why you have called your sister tonight, where is she? I would like to meet her.”

I made some noises, which made my sister alert; she came out with a stick, just to find no one. I was really irritated now. I decided I won’t tell it to anyone. I would handle it myself. My sister left my room after some time. We waited, but no one was there. She told me to call her if there is anything and she left.

After few minutes of her leaving, he came appeared again.

He opened the notebook and says, “Why are you having so much doubts, it’s me only, the one who spoke to you. I had told you that I would be back, now that am back you do not believe me. What should I do to make you believe me?” I didn’t say anything, I just look at him. Somewhere I felt he was saying truth.

He said, “I want you to take somewhere, will you come with me?” I look at him with doubt, he says, “You can trust me, I will never cause any harm to you. I promise you that and I also promise that I would take utmost care of you at any cost. “He lend his hand to me, and I don’t know I was lost in his eyes, I felt what he said was true. I move forward, I could see something coming to me, it was all powders.

I faint with the smell of it, and I don’t understand what happened. I could see I was not in my body; I was out of it, standing next to him.

He was smiling, he said, “I know, am sorry, I needed to do this, it is for your good. Come along princess.” Saying so he held my hands. I wasn’t in my senses; I was feeling dizzy like any moment I would faint. He took my hand and

I had this drunk type of feeling. I don't really remember what happened.

Chapter Three

I felt as if I was flying, as if I was loose. I have read that when we go in outer space we tend to float, and in the same manner, I felt as if I was floating, as if all my weight was gone. I wondered if this was journey he was talking about; if it was then I don't want to return.

Suddenly he held me closer, I could feel his breathe on my ears, his hands were around me, we were standing now, he lifted his hands towards my eyes, closed my already close eyes and whispered in my ears softly while removing his hands from my eyes, " Open your eyes slowly princess."

I did as instructed, he was still standing close to me, I looked to the view in front of me, I was amused , it was a palace, just like the ones which I had drawn. He held my hand again, was smiling at me; I look to him still in confusion. As we walked in, the palace seemed even more beautiful, though it had demolished large extent. He took me to even larger room, and asked me to change my clothes. He gave me something which looked like salwar, there were jewellery as well. I wasn't a fan of all these so when he gave me I gave him an is-it-needed look and he smiled and went out. I observed the room, it was huge, very huge, but I wondered where are we, why is this place so empty, what is actually going on, where have I landed. I thought of my home too, they would be worried, though they wouldn't notice my absence, because I was mostly in my room, only when I needed something I came out, but yet I know they would be worried, how will I inform them, what would I tell them of where I was, would they believe my story even if I told them, thinking all these I changed to this new attire. It felt as if something was telling me to do all these; I didn't want to change, but having that powder like thing was making me suffocated.

I went out; he smiled and again held my hands. He took me to the table, were food was ready. I didn't like the food which was kept in the table. He was very happy I could make out from his face. I was hungry but I couldn't really eat those things kept in front. Finally I saw fruits, which made me bit relieved. I ate a bit, curiosity started killing me, I wanted to ask and I felt like I could, I opened my mouth and voice came, for the first time. I was shocked, I couldn't move, I touch my throat in disbelief. I try to make noise again, I could hear my voice. I get up from the table and walk. He came behind me, calling out something, I didn't bother to wait, and he came in front of me and blocked my way.

He broke his silence finally and said, "Don't be shocked, you can speak now."

I looked at him and after few moments I said, "How did this all happen? What's happening?"

He looked at me and said, "You can say thank you first, instead of asking questions. "

I smiled looking all around, I went towards the window, it was beautiful outside, and I had never seen such a lovely sight ever in my life.

He came near me and said, "How do you find it here? "

I looked at him in confusion, and I asked again, "Tell me what is all this about, I wouldn't have shared my secrets had I known a man was hidden in it."

He laughed and said, "Well, now I do know and it's not secret, I actually fell in love with you ages ago. "
Now I felt like he was going too weird, so I asked him, "It's already very weird, don't make it even weirder." He smiled again.

He came towards me and said, "How strange it is, we don't even know each other's name, am Adnan, what about you? "

I was feeling nice as I never got this chance to say my name before anyone, so I said with smile, "I am Maya."
He looked at me in eyes again, I don't really know what this feeling was, and my heart and brain was too confused. Whenever I looked at him in his eyes I felt something, like something is there between us which connected us. I always wondered what the feeling of love be like, was it this which was happening to me, I was not just attracted but also awestruck with his charm. This feeling didn't really come to Jai, whom I claimed to be in love with.

He asked me to sit in big chair which was there near the window, he came with me, he sat next to me, and then I asked him, "Where are we? Which place is this?"

He looked outside the window and told me, "Where do you think it is?"

I just went blank, he said, "This was once paradise on earth, called, well am not sure if you have even heard about it, this existed years ago and we don't belong anymore here. I don't know what the name is now".

I was still confused if I really got my voice, so I said, "Do you mind if I scream?"

He laughed on it and said, “You can do whatever you want to do, there is no one to say anything to you princess.” I screamed at the top of my voice, laughed, sang, told my name many times.

Once I got hold of myself I asked him again, “Tell me your story now and how did you become a pen?”

He looked down and said, “It might sound weird for you as its old story but that is truth. Long back we used to practice magic, it was used for both good and bad. I was born prince, this is my palace, used to be, now it is like this, earlier there used to be so many people here, people were different in those times, they were more human than animal, it was really like heaven. I had very less interest in learning what a princes normally learn, I was more into arts, I wanted to learn how to read and write, and tried my best to share it to people. I loved singing and all other forms of art.”

He stopped there and said, “Come here, have to show you something.”

We went through another hallway towards another room, that room was even bigger, he said, “This used to be my room. I hated wars, one such time when we were on war with another kingdom, as always I had hidden away, I was scared of blood.” He was silent, he said after a while, “I ran towards some other place, I wasn’t a warrior, my brothers used to make fun of me a lot. I couldn’t do anything. Amongst the trees I saw a young lady, I felt like she was dancing. I could only see her eyes, it was too sharp and powerful. She wasn’t dancing, she was practising with her sword. In a while she sat down, she slowly removed her shawl from her eyes, which fell from her face, she was very beautiful. She started singing, it was the loveliest voice I had ever heard. “There was silence again, he continued, “I joined her singing but suddenly she stopped singing and left, she was furious but then she turned back and smiled shyly." He stopped speaking; he was looking outside as if he was in search of words.

I was completely lost in the story, I said, "Then what happened?"

He looked at me and just smiled, I said again, "This sounds so much like movie, was this really happened?"

He smiled and said, "I made it like this so it's much easier for you to understand. "

Someone entered the room, and said something in some other language.

He winked at me and said, "Come with me, someone wants to meet you."

I was surprised, who would I know here. I go with him, it seemed just like my sketch, it was fully built of stone. I see an old man and lady in front of me, they smile at me, and I smile back.

The old woman comes to me, and hugs me and says, "Oh my Aisha, you are finally back, it took so much time for you to come back here, now everything will be fine soon. I am so happy today."

I was looking at her confusingly. The old man was kind of furious, he asked me, "Where were you all these time?"

I look at everyone with confused look. I slightly nudge him asking him what is this, he smiles and says, "We will meet you at dinner." They both smile and we leave there place. On the way back, there are so many servants who kept bowing.

I was feeling so strange. I ask again, "What is happening? Who is Aisha? I am not Aisha. Where would I be?"

He turned back and said, "I didn't complete it, there is a reason why you are here, I will tell you, come." I follow him.

We reach his room again, he asks me to sit down.

He says, "So as I was saying. " I wasn't interested to listen to his story though now, as I could see it was snowing. I had never seen snowfall in my life.

I say, "Am sorry to interrupt, but can we please go out, I want to see snowfall."

He smiles and says, "You haven't changed after all these years."

I say "Stop it dude, come lets go." He takes me outside. It is not a crowded place. Once I reached outside, I started playing in the snowfall. It felt nice. It was just snowing mildly, slightly cold.

Someone came in between, another old woman, she came and said, "Aisha darling, it's so good to see you, how are you now? Save us, our queen." I looked at her in confusion, I say, "I think we should leave, am getting scared."

He said something to her and to me he said, "Are you sure?" I nod, we come back to the same room. I say, "Please help me, am really scared. "

I want to go home." He said, "This is your home. Don't be scared, I will let you go once you free Aisha."

I was like what the hell is this now, I say, "Stop it Okay, enough of jokes. How will I free Aisha?" He says, "You will come to know."

I say, "Okay, now tell me what happened after that?"

He looked outside, and continued. "We met the next day also, I didn't have courage to go a speak to her. I just looked at her, she came and spoke to me, and she knew I was a prince. She asked me why was I not at the war, she said if she was a man she would be there. I told her I have no interest in the war, I want to teach people how to read and write, like I know. As the days passed by, we became good friends, she was an art lover like me, and she used to draw sketches on the sand. The whole time when there was a war, morning and night, we were together. Slowly, our friendship turned to love. But by then, war had got over. We had to leave battlefield. So, preparations were going on, I met my future wife, those days things were lot more weird than it is now, she was a normal woman, her dreams were limited, and I didn't feel anything towards her, she was beautiful, very beautiful, actually, but I had no interest in her beauty. I made time to go back to forest in the midst of these preparations. Marriages were much more grand affairs before, especially if you are prince. I broke the news of marriage to her, she was sad, but didn't show anything, that's one thing I never understood about women, you are all so unique; I left that day with heavy heart. Somehow in the end things worked in my favour. I got married to my love. But sometimes past can fall heavy. I was a womanizer. I was driven by lust and hence I had favourite, her name was Sana. If I hadn't met her, I gave my word to her that I would marry her."

I don't why but then I interrupted, I said, " You lived happily ever after and decades later your son or daughter fell in love with that persons son or daughter and you guys met after long time and all that?"

He looked at me furiously and said, "Why are you so impatient? Why don't you like love? Normally the people who like reading have so many fantasies about love."

I laughed and said, "Yeah, its fantasies not reality, there is a whole lot of difference, and it's nice to read about it in books, not in reality."

He came bit closer to me and said, "That is because you have never been in love, then you would understand how beautiful it is."

I got bit furious on that, how could he say that, I said, and "Who told you that? I am in love with Jai."

He laughs and says, "Seriously, you only found that guy? "

I say, "You don't know him, why are you saying this."

He says, "I know him too, you also know him, you just don't remember what happened. He is not a good person. He doesn't love you he is just using you."

I was angry again, I said, "How will you know that? "

He said, "You will come to know."

I didn't reply to this statement, well, to be honest, he was right, I wasn't in love with Jai, I was too desperate to be in love and experience it that I had said yes to him, but I was sort of attracted to this person in front of me , who in a way happens to be a ghost.

He said, continuing the story, "That's not what happened, I was hardly interested in my marriage or anything related to that, I never wanted to have a family. I just wanted to taste all flavours of lust. Every women is different and so is there way of making love. I knew I had to change, I was ready to change as well but somewhere my devil was still alive. I was more attracted to Sana than to my love. I had to stop it. I saw her on the forest one day when I went for hunting. I went towards her and made love to her, for the very first time I touched her. Even though I had made love to many women, this seemed different. I felt like now I was making love to a woman. Every part of her was unique. We made love and it felt as if everything had become complete now." He had tears in his eyes as he said so, the way his voice went was something adorable, he is perfect gentleman, maybe because he is a prince, for a moment I wished I lived in such time, but then whatever time it was its always bad for a woman.

I said seeing his silence, “What happened after that? “ He looked at me with his teary eyes. We hear a knock again in the door. Someone tells that someone had come to meet me. I don’t want to go out because I don’t know what to say as it am not me.

I ask, “What am I supposed to do now, who has come to meet me?” He says, “Don’t worry princess, am there with you, nothing can happen, just do as I say.”

I nod. We leave to another place, it is huge corridor and then there is this we can say an auditorium. There were people so many of them, all looked like the ones in old times. I was feeling so heavy. Everyone was bowing down as I was walking. The strange thing is it was all like the sketches I had drawn. Every single thing was same, it made me scared. In the end there was this seat which I had seen in pictures and normally in movies which depicted history, a huge chair, or the crown seat. It was too huge, we were led there. Suddenly someone came and pulled something, it was like a partition, or a curtain not sure but suddenly we were like in a separate room. An old lady came from inside, she came towards with teary eyes. I was looking at all in confusion.

She said, “My child, what have you become now, come here with me.”

I said, “Where? What has happened to me?”

She nodded sadly and said, “I knew you will ask, there is only death of bodies not of souls. You always were like this, you had so many questions to ask and you wouldn’t leave if you didn’t get an answer. Good old times. Come with me.”

I went with her, it looked very strange. She asked me to sit and close my eyes. She applied something when I closed my eyes. I could sense that some gel sort thing was applied to my forehead. She asked me to open my eyes, and I could feel changes happening in me, I was hearing noises all over like someone screaming for help. People laughing, calling out names. It all seemed weird for me to understand. I could see a womanly figure but I wasn't sure who it was. I could see him far and saying something unrelated.

I hated those gaps when he was telling the story, I wanted to know what happened but he was taking so much time. He looked at me and held my hands to another big room. He said, "This is where she used to be, her favourite place."

He came closer to me, holding me from back. I felt weird because I never experienced this kind of touch from anyone. His breathes were on my ears, making me shiver. I was just standing there not knowing what to do.

He said, "I don't know how much you will believe or how much I can convey it to you, it's an age old story and bit complicated. There are magicians involved, I have no idea for what, even now I don't know and I don't want to know either."

A drop of tear fell as he said this. I was out of words, for I didn't want to be Aisha, no way.

I looked at him and asked, "What are you trying to say?"

He looked at me and smiled, "Let me release my pain princess, the story is not yet over. "

I said, "Okay, go on, complete the story."

He said, "One day as I was in my room, suddenly I was being taken away to some other place. It was filled with so many women, I got lost in between them. Sana came in and she gave me something to drink. I don't know what happened after that. I had become so lusty, all I could see was having pleasure. I was just enjoying everything. I even became violent which made me kill one of the women. She was very beautiful. Sana was aware of my marriage. She didn't want it to happen. She made me promise her again that I will only marry her, till then she wouldn't release me. I didn't agree. She would come and ask me something or she would make me do something with someone. My family got the news that there mad son is being taken as captive in brothel. They knew it was some black magic which she had cast on me. They summoned magician in the palace. The only thing bothering me was Aisha, I was sure it was something related to her which made all these. I was released from chains, when this was going on, my Aisha was already dead by then. The magician who was brought by my family had won but then timing was a problem, the precious magic trick had already started working, and now what can be done is to reverse it and to make it less , so they told me that when I come into right hands, I will get my ability to speak and I could be released, and for that I had to bring that person to the palace, which may or may not exist, to the same place and to live with that person for seven days as king and queen, or in simple words we should meet and live seven days in peace then our curse will end and we shall be united forever."

The way he narrated his story made me even have tears in my eyes, but I still had questions so I asked him, "What if a guy used the pen or what if the ink just spilled out of it?"

He said to this, " Before you, I was passed on to many people, everyone kept me in nice shelves, as some treasure, no one even opened , you are the only one held it in your hands, and you are good with words."

I looked at him and said, "So are you trying to say that am Aisha?"

He smiled shyly and said, "No princess, you are not Aisha, but yes my Aisha lives in you."

I didn't understand that and asked him again, "Is there anything I can do to help you?" He looked here and there and said, "You know you are my wife."

I just looked at him with what-the-fuck expression and he smiled again and said, " Don't look like that, I know it's all huge confusion for you, but you have the body of my wife and soul of Aisha, Sana never forgave me, I don't blame her. But I can never accept her as my wife. Aisha will leave me if I accepted Sana. I don't want to lose Aisha at any cost. Both of them loved me and there love caused all this. If only I was a nice person. But I guess, it took too much time for me to be human. "

I understood where the story was going to, and his description of love made me feel like being in love, but I know it is not possible. I asked him again, "How is that possible? I don't want to make out with a ghost. "

He laughed on this and said, "No princess you are getting it wrong, there is just one thing which has to be done, come with me." He took my hands and I have no idea where we were going, we walked between huge trees, it was so beautiful.

Chapter Four

He took me to a cave where we saw a very old person, we went inside and on seeing us the old man said, "You have come, I have been waiting for you all these time." He looked like hermit, and he looks bit scary too, he was looking at me so much I got scared and went behind him, hiding myself. He asked me to come forward and instructed me to sit down. I sat down and he applied some powder in my throat, after applying that though, some changes happened in my body. I was someone else now. I wasn't too thin but neither was I fat, but I was bit huge. I had pimples in my face and I never really bothered about my looks. For a girl in her 20s it is big thing but for me I wasn't at all interested in all these stuff. I was nerd in all ways. I don't know what happened, I felt as if I had become someone else, the old man smiled and said, "Now you will have a voice, and you shall do whatever you are destined to do."

We left the place, while walking back it seemed as if I was walking through known places. I was able to recognize all these places. I had never been to these places till now but I could slowly remember. I held his hands more tightly. As we were walking I went towards him and out of some intense emotions, brushed his hair with my fingers, looked at his eyes, went more close towards him, and kissed him. I haven't kissed anyone so far, and I didn't know how to kiss, but it just came, it was long kiss, we kissed till we became breathless. He hugged me and I hugged him back and I had tears in my eyes and I could sense he also had tears.

He cupped my face in his hand and said, " Aisha, jaanum, finally we are together." I smiled shyly and we walked back to the palace.

I could remember each of the things which had happened. I know this man, he is my love. I felt like I woke up from a long sleep, as if I was brought back to this world again to life again. We went back to the palace, he invited me to another room, gave me another dress, another set of ornaments. When I came out, he took me to mirror, I looked like someone else, and I had changed from Maya to someone else.

He said, "You look so beautiful, am so happy that I can't express in words."

I turned towards him, and held his hands and said, "Don't ever leave me. I have been searching for you all these time,"

He smiled again and said, "We shall be together always." He held me in his arms and brushed my hair gently.

I withdrew his hold and asked him, "But I don't belong here, I will have to go back, what would happen then?"

He brushed my hair and said, "It took centuries for me to find you, do you think I will leave you now? You will have to return but I shall be with you always, don't worry."

He held me again in his arms, brushing my hair with his fingers, though we were madly in love before, we never had the courage to be in each other's arms, all the love was through eyes, now the time has reached were we could be what we are without being afraid. He was a strong man, he looked really handsome, the most handsomest and charming person I had ever seen till now. I believe maybe that's why I never liked anyone till now, maybe because my love was always with me though I was unaware of it. I was having long hair now, my hair was short, and lot of physical changes happened I was looking beautiful. I now understood why I had always felt some sort pain as if I had lost something all my life, I had everything required to be happy but I wasn't happy. I guess this was that missing thing in my life. I had shut myself away from everyone and everything, I had this rebellion and revenge inside me but I didn't know what it was against. I always behaved as if am going through a break up.

He came from my back and held me again, and said, "What happened, is everything alright? What are you thinking about?"

I looked back and smiled, and remained silent.

He held my hands and took me towards sofa, asked me to sit there, he sat near to me and said, " I was there in front of you, but unless you were ready I couldn't come before, you always said, you were hurt, you cried most of the days, and I used to see you every day, I saw you crying yourself to sleep, I wanted to come and hold you close and say it will be fine, I was dying in that pen too. Tell me jaan, why were you crying? "

I looked down and said, "I actually don't know, most of the times I felt like shouting whenever people showed me sympathy, I never wanted that, I just wanted someone to hear me, to understand my silence, no one would, I never had any friend, with whom I could share anything, I was always alone. I wanted to sing, I couldn't, I love to sing poetry but that too I can't." He stood up and came towards me and hugged me, I was crying.

He said,"Shh...it's okay...it's all thing of a past, you can do whatever you want to do now, I will make sure, you are able to do anything you want to do."

He wiped my tears and said, "You have such beautiful smile jaan why are you not using it, common smile now."

I started smiling and laughing. We had bit of conversations but most of the times we were just looking into each other's eyes.

Suddenly I break the silence, I ask him, "What is happening in my house? Can I go back to meet my family?"

He said, "Yes of course, we will return together, don't worry, for now just be here, don't think about anything else." I smiled and then we had food again, I was feeling weird, wearing all those heavy dresses. Most of the time we were silent, it felt strange talking too, for I am not used to it.

I said after a while, "I never knew I will get a chance to visit Kashmir like this, not this place has become more favourite. But why is it that we don't see anyone else, nearby."

He gave a naughty smile and said, "You have so many questions, this palace doesn't actually exist, it's far from the world, magic destroyed this palace, and people belonging here and that's the reason we are not known to any people, there are people who come to search, they come and go, but normal people don't come here, you know the current state of things, politics and all, things have fallen miserably. Earlier it was a paradise on earth."

I looked at him every time with more admiration. I had fallen in love, I don't know who I was Aisha or Maya but whoever I was I had fallen for this man, and there is nothing I could do about it. I loved the way he spoke, the way he looked at me, the way he called me princess, the way he held me, everything. I smiled and on seeing that he also smiled. It just felt magical whenever our eyes met.

I asked him after having food, "So from where does all these food and dishes come? Who cooks it?"

He said, "Magic, I also know bit of magic, I had arranged everything, you remember when I left a note that I would be back, I came here and arranged everything."

I said, "Oh that's really nice."

He held my hands again and we went for walk at night, it was beautiful. Moon shined brighter, mountains were shining, and trees were sparkling. It was amazing. As we were walking, he held me close to him, holding each other. I felt so safe. We returned back in a while, he played some music, the kind which I like, he said it was his favourite too, after he while he gave his hand and invited me to dance with him. It was a slow track , he held be by my waist, and by one hand he was brushing my hair, he was singing too, and in sometime I started singing the same song. I didn't knew which song it was or which language it was, I started to sing along him , looking at his eyes, we were moving very slowly.

We were so lost in each other's eyes, that we didn't stop singing, he came closer and kissed my eyes, saying, "Your eyes are the prettiest eyes I have ever seen."

He kissed my nose, my cheeks and then he kissed my lips. It was long passionate kiss. Slowly he took me in his arms, I didn't know where he was taking me, and all I could see was his eyes. He put me in the bed as if I were his child, held my head softly and kept me in pillow. He started kissing me again, with each kiss, each cell of my body came alive. He caressed me so much, in a way I haven't ever felt. All I could see was the love which was waiting to be given. As moments passed by, slowly , he came to me, it wasn't lust neither pain nor pleasure, it was just love and maybe the so called act of love making didn't feel like anything so great as people exaggerate it felt much higher and above it, because we just one emotion and that was love. He touched my body with his fingers, his fingers were moving so smoothly, I was feeling ticklish. I was feeling shy. He started removing my clothes one by one. It was feeling weird. He started kissing me slowly again. Our lips were twirling. He went on kissing my neck, slowly held my breasts. His lips touched one of my breasts, I gave a small moan. He started sucking them more, my fingers played through his hairs, holding him tightly. He went further down, kissing my belly. He was kissing, sucking and licking me, I had started moaning more now. He had removed his dress as well in this process. He kissed my inner thighs, I wasn't really prepared for this much. I was wet to a great extent. I was flowing with juices I could say in other words. He inserted his fingers on my wet pussy. He started rubbing, I was biting my lower lips and almost screaming.

He stopped for a moment. He started licking my pussy so madly, I don't even know how to describe it. First of all it was the first time I was making out with anyone. He came up to me again, we were kissing so madly. I didn't know when but he had inserted his dick on my still wet pussy. I did get an orgasm when he was licking. We were kissing and at the same time, he was getting more and more into me. I did feel pain in the beginning, but the kiss I guess worked. My fingers kept wandering through his broad back. He had increased the speed from being gentle, it became sort of aggressive. He went on and on, kept on giving me orgasms. It was as if he didn't want to leave me, he just wanted to be inside me. I was tired after a while. I don't know when but I had slept off in his arms.

He was gentle, just like he seemed, there weren't really much of difference between him and me. He came closer to me, held me in his arm closely, and with every his all, he gave I took it with even more love. I felt as if I were a flower going to bloom. He made the woman in me alive. Our breathes smelled similar, our smiles looked similar, our eyes looked similar, and our love above all was even more similar. I didn't realize when the night had gone and morning came, I had seen mornings before also, but this morning, I was wrapped in his arms, he was playing with my hairs, gently smiling on me, kissing on my forehead every now and then, whispering at times.

Chapter Five

I opened my eyes and he said, “Princess.”

He kissed me again, and I smiled shyly, he came down to my face again and kissed. We kissed again, every time we kissed, we didn’t want to leave each other’s embrace. I withdrew myself after some more sessions of kissing, cuddling and love making and again dosed off to sleep. I woke up after a while and when I searched for him, he was no were to be found, I felt scared, real scared and that’s when I realized what mistake I have done and what trouble I have got myself into. I got up, wore my clothes back, ran throughout the palace, couldn’t find any way out, neither could find any person to ask for help. I wished to run out, and I went each way was confusing.

After running a while, I bumped onto him, he held me and asked, “What happened? Why do you look so scared?”

I just smiled and said, “I thought I lost you again. “

He held me in his arms and said,” That will never happen again.” Just as he said that, there was loud noise, and we could see some figure, but couldn’t really figure out who it was, it came near to us, taking shape of woman.

She stood in front of us, and started laughing, she came close to me, and when she did he held me even closer.

She came forward and said laughing, "Love birds, why, how dare you, what does she have that I don't have, didn't I love you?"

He looked at me and said, "I didn't say that you lacked anything."

She took a close look on us and started doing something with her hands which I didn't understand. It was like a battle of wind. So much wind and dust flew. He asked me to move back, he was fighting and protecting me at the same time. The fight went on, he in the end had to put the sword in her head. The enemy was finally dead. He came and cupped my face and said, "Half of our work is over."

I didn't understand what he was saying or what was actually happening, was I alive or dead? He led me to another door way, there were large windows, I could see the it was autumn season, one of the most beautiful seasons. I had so many questions, but I really didn't know where to start.

After walking a while, in order to get hold of the situation, asked him, "Can we go out for some time, just get some fresh air?"

He didn't respond, just walked, and I walked behind him, after a while, he said, "Close your eyes princess." I closed my eyes, I could feel gentle breeze touching me, and in a while, he wrapped me again in his arms, and said, "Now slowly open your eyes." I opened my eyes, capturing the beauty, it was so beautiful, and it just seemed as if another scenery had really become alive.

I was so lost in the beauty, we stood there still for some time. After a while I said, "Why don't we go out, just take a walk."

He withdrew himself and said, "Okay, as you command my princess."

I didn't like why he called me princess all the time. I do have a name. I was so confused, I felt as if my brain would burst any minute. One end I was Aisha, who was his lover, one end I was Maya, the numb girl. I had lost my identity. I didn't hate Maya but I didn't love her either, maybe it is for the best. We went outside, it was just so beautiful. There were huge trees, and in between fallen leaves. The way leaves moved in the ground, with music of wind, it seemed as if it was dance. We went towards bench and sat there. I could always catch him looking at me stealing glances on which I would smile. It seemed as if I was acting in some old movie. I wanted to know more, so I decided I should frame questions in a way he wouldn't feel bad. He started humming some strange song to which birds came and even birds started to sing in that tune.

After that, I asked him, "Why have I never read or heard your name in history or any other books?"

He laughed and said, "There are many stories which were never told by anyone, are you having doubts now? What happened?"

I felt bad, maybe I had hurt him who I didn't want so I said, "No it isn't that, am quite confused, past and present is driving me nuts. I don't understand to where I belong, what am I doing, where am going to, what is this whole about. I don't really understand and am really going crazy."

He took my hands and kissed my palm and held it tight and said, "Be it past or present, you belong to me, and this is about just you and me, it has been and it will always be."

It felt nice hearing those words, but I was getting concerned now, what was actually happening to me, I couldn't control it I said, " I know, it feels nice, I can speak now, I have voice, I can sing and I am in love but can you please tell me what is going to happen next? Will we be just here? Why aren't there any people here? "

He looked down and said, "I can't tell you the whole story of the curse, remember this though that I will never let anything happen to you, we are in I guess Kashmir as it is known now, and in present context you are no longer in India, you will return soon back to your place in some time, there aren't people here because we are not visible to anyone, neither can we see them." I felt more confused hearing it, and bit scared as well. Where are we in real, I couldn't imagine me being in other side. I felt really nervous now. I needed a way out.

I started crying, I had made love to a ghost. What would Jai think of me when he comes to know that I had slept with someone else? I was no longer a virgin. I had made a mistake. I started panicking. How did I believe this person, for what reasons did I think he was telling the truth.

He came near me, I got up and said, "Who do you think you are? How dare you do all this to me?"

He was looking at me in confusion, I said, "You think all this magic stories I will believe? It is all non-sense. You lied to me."

He was still calm, he said, "I can understand but tell me then how did you draw me? Check your sketches, you had drawn this castle before also. "

I say, "It was from imagination."

He smiles and says, "This is also imagination then."

I look at him with confusion, he says, "I was being nice with you, and this is how you behave with me? Who told you to draw me? I was happy in my world."

I give him a disgusted look and walk away, he comes behind me and holds my hand. He says, "You think you can leave this place?"

I had made a huge mistake and I have no idea how I am going to correct it. He says, "Look I have nothing against you, but you know you released me, but still I can't let you go so easily. "

He was just murmuring words, I realized there is something wrong with him. I go near him and say, "You can share if there is something bothering you. Maybe I can help you out."

He looks at me and says, "I wish so."

I ask, "What do you mean?" He takes a sigh and says, "I am sorry I had lied to you, it wasn't my story. It is something different. You are nice person and I don't cause harm to people with good heart."

I was blushing hearing this, I said, "So if that is not your story then what your story is, maybe I can help."

He looks outside the window and says, "I don't know, it isn't that easy as you think. I have been cursed. I am very lusty person. I desire to be in bed all the time. I was born as a prince, and everyone hated me here because I was all the time in brothels. For me it was like if I wanted someone I got that person. No one ever objected because I would shower them with money or jewellery or whatever they asked. It is in that time when I was out for hunting I came across this beautiful lady, she was not like the normal ladies. She was practising with her sword and in those times it is not allowed for women to fight. She removed her shawl slowly from her eyes. I was awestruck with her beauty. She had sharp eyes, she started singing. I was in total love with her voice. I came back every day to see her. I had lost interest in other women, for she ruled my brain all the time. I had given my word to a lady named Sana that I will be here forever, she was my favourite in the brothel. I was sure that she would never like a person like me even if I am prince. I didn't hold a good name. I was always under the influence of alcohol or drugs. I had slowly stopped that, I got myself in the track of good. Everyone was confused. Even my family members started respecting me a bit for it was good change. I told my father that I wanted to marry her, he didn't say anything , maybe he knew no one would give me there daughter. He told me that if they agree you can. I went and asked her father, he didn't agree. But she did, she liked me I don't know why. I got married to her and I had changed more, she was my inspiration. I had become king in all ways. Sana on the other hand was furious. She took help of black magic to control her anger to both of us. She tried her best to bring me back to my old ways, but I wouldn't go. Even if she made me do things, in the last moment I would just go from there. She went and took resort of black magician. Aisha had a very kind heart, she would always help anyone. One day one of servants gave a drink, it was told to her that it is juice, she drank it and within some time she lost her voice. Slowly, she started losing everything, her hair, eye sight, she was bed ridden. One day, she passed away. I could never accept it that she was no more. I went to depression and I was more into all these than before. Sana was happy, I told her she would be my queen now. One day one of the girls told me that it was all her doing to be the queen. I got furious and I went to her, she tried to calm me down but it didn't happen. She applied something on my head, it made me turn into a lustful beast. I would just be behind every woman in kingdom. My family was really fed up with me by now. They called someone to get me in control. He tied me with ropes and all and applied something in my head. I felt really heavy, I felt dizzy and I fainted. After that I was kept in bottle. My family members were sad yet they were relieved. After some time, I would turn out to be a pen that is the second part of the curse which she had cast. When the pen comes to the rightful hand I shall be free. I shall be free from the curse."

I look at him, he was telling the truth I felt so. I say, "So you mean now you are free? "

He smiles and says, "Yes, somewhat I am free, I just told you two parts of the curse, there is a third part as well. I need to make love to you for seven nights, this will make me and Aisha free from the spell."

I became numb. I didn't know what to tell him, I just looked at him, and I felt like I would vomit any moment. He gave me water to drink. I drank it in one go.

After calming myself down, I said, "Are you even aware of what you just told, look everything is fine but the last one I can't accept it, what would become of me then? I don't want to make out with you at least. What would happen to me after that you even thought of it?"

He took a sigh and said, "You came here trusting me right? Trust me for little more time, I promise nothing will happen to you. I will make sure of that you return home safe and you will be with the person you love. This will be forgotten with time."

I don't know for what stupid reason but I still trusted this person.

I ask, "Promise?"

He smiled and nodded. I asked, "What are we supposed to do then? Just this?"

He laughs and says, "No obviously not. Come here, let's go have some food first."

We went towards the hall way, there were too many people waiting for us. All were smiling and waving at us. I felt like I was in some sort of fairy tale movie. We went to have food, it was too good. I have never tasted such delicious food ever in my life. He had made sure it is all vegetables. I felt bit nervous of what was to follow. This would be our first night. I don't know if what happened previously would be counted. I was introduced to many people. All of them addressed me as Aisha. After the gathering, I was taken to another room. It had huge bed, it seemed old though. I was looking all around, it felt as if it was one of the rooms in museums.

I ask him, "Why haven't I heard about this anywhere till now."

He gave a naughty smile and said, "There is things in history like that which no one knows. The people whom you met where your parents, centuries ago. The moment you released me this palace became alive again. This would go when you leave. The whole place."

I looked at him, and said, "Isn't this Kashmir?"

Chapter Six

He laughed and said, “No, you assumed it to be, I don’t know where this belongs now.” I went towards the window, it was still snowing. I was lost in the beauty of the snow when I could feel someone hands moving through my waist. His hands came slowly through both the sides of my waist. He slowly blew air to my ears and kissed them slowly. It made me feel ticklish.

He started licking my ear lobes. After a while he bit it slowly which made me moan a bit. He started to hold my waist more strongly. I turned towards him, he cupped my face and starting kissing me on my cheeks, eyes and slowly he took in my lips. He sucked my lips as if he was going to remove it. I did not know what to do. He took me towards the bed as we kissed. He placed me slowly on bed and started kissing me more. He wasn’t getting enough of it I guess. I was wearing a gown that day. I had removed the shawl from my body once we were in the room. He was on top of me when we were kissing. His hands wanted to reach towards the zip to open my gown. I wasn’t letting that happen. Whenever his hands went back I was holding his hands more, making us kiss more deep. He turned me back side and opened the zip. He was getting aggressive. He started kissing my back, I had started moaning like crazy.

He turned me to front again, removing the gown from my body. He was looking at my breasts now. I could feel my nipples had become really hard now. He caressed them, and held them tightly. He then started sucking one of them, while he sucked one, he pressed the other one very hard. I had started screaming now. He didn't stop sucking. He kept on sucking and on between he would pinch them too. I was so aroused by now. He got up after that and came to me again kissing me on my lips. He had removed his dress as well in the meantime. I didn't notice it when he did that but I could feel his bare skin on me now. He went down after that to my belly. He kissed my belly and pressed my belly button so hard, that I moaned loud again. He started licking belly button after that holding my breasts. I pulled his hair as reaction.

He came towards my shoulders after that, kissing my neck and he came to my arms. He went on kissing my fingers. His hands were playing through my legs. He came down after that, kissing my legs. His hands wandered through my thighs first. He spread my legs wide, and started kissing my inner thighs. I was moaning so much, the only thing which I was saying was "Ahhh-aahhh-Ahhhh-ohhh". I have only heard this before when I watched porn not in real life. He looked at me for a moment, and inserted his two fingers on my wet pussy. I moaned in pain. He started rubbing so fast. He took his fingers out, and started licking my wet pussy. I was going crazy. I felt as if I could orgasm any time, but he wouldn't let that happen. Whenever I was about to get, he would do something else. He widened my legs more now and let my hands touch his dick. It had become so hard. He clasped my hands tight after that. He inserted his dick onto my wet pussy so swiftly that I didn't know when he had come in me. He slowly started going up and down, clasping my hands and kissing me badly. I wasn't getting gap even to moan. He increased his speed and I was going crazy. He was going up and down on too fast.

The whole bed was shaking now. It felt as if he was in me completely. Our breathes had increased, my heart beats were increasing with each time he moved. He had removed his hands from clasp, he was pinching my breasts. I was biting his neck and my hands wandered in his back. He increased the speed more, I was moaning so loudly now. I think it aroused him more when I moaned. He also started to moan. He took out his dick in between and again inserted it more inside. He went going in and out sometimes up and down. I got an orgasm, my breathes calmed down now, heart beats were still at high speed, even that calmed down. He was still inside me, he came slowly towards my chest and placed his lips there, it felt as if he was kissing my heart. I held him close in my arms.

He was still in me, he came up and kissed me on my lips. I was tired, really tired.

He said, "Are you okay?"

I said, "Yeah, I am sleepy."

My body was paining, I just wanted to sleep. I don't know when I woke up, when I opened my eyes, I saw him sitting on the chair.

He came towards me when he saw me awake, he said, "You awake."

I just smiled. He caressed my hair.

I said, "What is the time now?"

He said, "It is around ten, why what happened?"

I said, "Is this going to be like this for the coming six days more?"

He laughed. I said, "I am just really drowsy and tired, never had something like this before. "

He nodded, he said, "It will get more, yesterday was our first night that is why it was just once, now on it is going to be from when sun goes down till sun is up."

My mouth was wide open hearing this, I said, "Am I sex slave or something?"

He laughed and said, "No jaan, you are my love. It is going to be fine."

I said, "I hope so."

I was feeling nervous now. Six more days I had to spend here with him, it is going to get wilder I guess. I didn't feel like going out, I was just in the room. I got up slowly and took bath. I could see marks on my body. I guess it is what everyone calls love bites. I changed my dress. After some time, food was brought for me, I had food little. I was getting the taste of his lips in my mouth still. He was there with me the entire time. He made sure I was comfortable. He talked to me, I was lost in his eyes.

He said, "Sun will go down in some time." I was like what the hell, just now I had waked up.

I was standing near the window, still in the hangover of last night. I said, "I can't do this, I need time."

He came towards me and kept his hands on my lips. We were just looking at each other's eyes. He was tricky. He just started kissing me out of nowhere. I guess he liked kissing. His kiss would never end. He kept his hand on my breast and starting pushing it. Slowly his hands went towards my legs. He removed the zip from back, still kissing. He removed his dress also. I didn't understand what type of dress it was. I was already naked, he also became naked. He lifted me bit, towards the wall. He inserted his dick without any warning. It was direct action today. He kept on going in and out of me, I wasn't moaning now. He started pinching my nipples as he increased speed, I couldn't control then. I started moaning. He was smiling as if he achieved something. He went on doing that, went on going in and out in great speed. He stopped, I was on his dick now.

He took me towards bed. I was on top of him. I had no idea what I was to do. We were still kissing. He slapped my butt cheeks. I moaned again. I started moving on his dick. I was going in and out. In between, he would slap my butt. He held my breast tightly as I was jumping on him. He was so aggressive now, I could feel it. He pulled me down and started going in and out very fast. I had got an orgasm. He stopped for a moment, and then went on again. He was going slowly, then again he started increasing speed. I was so drowsy. I could see his face coming close nothing else. He kissed my neck and asked me to kneel down. I did as he instructed. He kissed my butt. He held my breasts tightly and inserted his dick from back. He started going more inside and inside. I fell on the bed when I got orgasm again. I didn't have strength to move.

I wasn't interested in this anymore, but I don't know if there was a way.

The next time I opened my eyes, he was sitting there waiting for me, I said, "Can we do one thing? "

He looked at me and said, "What?" I said, "I will just be on bed, you do whatever you want to. I am just too tired for going out and all. Just two days have passed, there is still five more days. "

He shrugged and said, "As you wish princess, just on the seventh day, you will need to dress up."

I said, "Okay."

I was full time on the bed. He would be there in the room with me, we would talk. He would feed me, I guess even I am in love with this person. He was kind, he used to talk to me all the time. At night though, he would turn to be opposite. He was very aggressive on bed. I don't even know how many times I got orgasms. Even though I was shy in the beginning, I had become no less. I was doing everything he wanted me to do. I had really become a sex slave. Four more days passed on very fast. He was very happy as the days passed by, somewhere I didn't want to leave this place. I was so comfortable with him.

As he said, the seventh day arrived. I wondered what would happen that day. He brought some very colourful dresses to me, and asked me to wear it. He gave me many ornaments as well. I looked like a bride. I know it wasn't me but I did look good. He took me to another room, it was decorated with flowers.

He said, "You look very beautiful today."

I said, "Only today?"

He laughed and said, "No, you know that."

Chapter Seven

I was looking all the sides, it wasn't like the other room, and this was bigger. I was feeling shy, I was looking down. He removed my shawl slowly from my head. His fingers ran through my hair. He kissed my cheeks first. I could sense he was too excited. He removed some of ornaments. He had also dressed up. He was looking really handsome. I swear I wished I was Aisha instead of Maya. He took me towards the bed. He cupped my face and planted soft kisses all over my face. He kissed me slowly, very slowly feeling my breathe and lips. He then moved his hands towards my breasts. I think he liked my breasts a lot. He would suck them for so long. He removed my dress very slowly. He kissed my neck, at some point he was licking my neck. I was feeling ticklish. My breasts were hard again.

Apart from having sex with a ghost, sleeping naked and wearing no winners were new to me. He pinched my breasts and started sucking them. I liked it when he sucked them. He was slow today though, he even bit them today. He would suck one and hold the other tight. I was already wet. He inserted his fingers on my pussy and started rubbing them slowly. He was still kissing me, while his fingers were playing on my pussy. He first rubbed hard, then he started rotating his fingers. I was moaning out loudly whenever I got a gap. He took his fingers out. He came up to me and put his dick on my cleavage, he was moving it hard. I was moaning. He then went down and widened my legs. He spread my pussy lips more and started licking. I was going crazy. I was just saying " ohm...ahhhhh.....mum....ohhhh...nooooo......ahhhhhh, ". Nothing else came out of me. He had dug his tongue deep in my pussy. He licked it more deep. He had reached my G-spot. My legs were still wide . He came up and inserted his hard dick on me. I moaned loud. He had come so deep tonight that I was confused what is mine and what is his. He started going in and out fast. It wasn't aggressive, he was very slow today. He went on doing that, he was kissing me while he went inside me. I got orgasm. As soon I got, I don't know what happened. The place turned out to be too bright. I couldn't see anything with brightness. A lady was standing there in front of me. She was looking at him, he was looking at her.

He hugged her as soon he saw her, she was smiling with tears in her eyes. They were touching each other as if they couldn't believe they were standing next to each other. He cupped her face and started kissing. She withdrew kiss in moment and hugged him again tightly. It felt like movie scene. I was there in the bed covered with blankets. I didn't know when he got himself covered up. After the initial hugging, kissing and sweet talks, he looked at me.

He said, " Jaan, this is Maya."

She came towards me and caressed my hair, she said, "Of course, I know her, I was in her for so long. Nice to meet you finally and I am sorry too for what happened. But what you did we will never ever forget."

I just smiled. I said, "So now it's all over? I can go back home?"

They both smiled and nodded.

I asked, “Will you guys take me back home?”

He came forward and said, “Of course princess, you did so much for me, I will do anything for you.”

I shrugged and said, “Yeah right, anything. You did so much and now that you got her back I am just anything.”

I don’t know what I was saying. I guess I got emotional. I was feeling jealous, I know it’s stupid.

I said, ’Now that you got what you wanted you will dump me right?”

She came and said, “No, we will come along with you.” I felt bit relieved now, that I will not be going alone.

I was still confused, where is the villain. I wanted to ask but then they were so busy already in each other that I thought not to ask anything, let it be. I look down at myself I could see I was wearing the same clothes with which I had come here, days ago. I remove the blanket, I wish I was still on his embrace like it used to be. I could hear sounds now, I don’t know from where, winds were blowing so fast. I saw a figure coming in front of me, it was a woman I guess. I couldn’t understand. They came next to me and both of them held my hands.

I took a closer look and saw it looked somewhat like Jai.

I turn to him and ask, “Why does this look like Jai?”

Aisha said, “ Maya, just like I was trapped in you , Sana is trapped in Jai. Now you need to rescue him as well just like you helped me out.”

I was like what non sense is this, still I was confused, and why was this such a confusing figure.

She came near Aisha and said, “You think you will get him now don’t you?” He came forward and said, “ Sana, let it be please, we had enough of problems now let us all live happily.”

Sana cum Jai started laughing loudly. I was getting scared, then he came and told me , " Princess, you need to go and kiss him when I tell you."

I said, " Why? For what? I slept with you for seven days, now you want this again? Why are you so driven by sex.?"

They all were looking at me, then I don't know if it's a she or he, came forward and said, " He uses everyone, he used you also , now see he went with her."

He got furious, he said, " I didn't use her, she agreed to help me, Maya, don't delay it."

I went near to the figure, I couldn't find lips. Somehow I found, I got hold of lips. I started kissing , I could feel something was happening on my behind. It felt as if there were fireworks going on behind. It seemed as if lights were all up. I just knew there were so much going on behind. Dark fumes were coming from Jai, as I kissed him, the fumes got thicker.

Aisha said, " Don't leave him, and keep going." It felt as if I was prince in fairy tale , who woke up princess from deep sleep. I was going breathless but I know if I stopped it would mean something bad will happen. I went on kissing till the dark fumes were completely gone. Jai pushed me back and was looking all around scared.

He looked at me and said, " Maya, Why are you here? How come you are here? Who are these people, are you okay?"

I said , " Relax, I will explain everything."

I still had voice, I thought it would be gone by now.

He said, " You can speak, oh my God, you can speak."

I was laughing and I screamed in joy. I could speak. I had voice.

Adnan came forward and said, " I don't know what to say, you have helped us so much, we are forever indebted to you. Now, all the dark clouds have cleared from our sky."

I was looking at him and at Jai. I felt relieved at least there was someone I knew.

I asked Jai, " What is happening in my house? Is everyone okay?"

He looked down and said, " They are sad, doctors said you were struck with lightning. You been unconscious from then, doctors said you are in coma."

I was surprised, I said, " Really? So I am there and I am here also, so what about you?"

He said, " I have no idea, what happened to me, I remember I was out then suddenly something hit then I am here."

I wanted to go home so badly, I wanted to see my sister and mother. They would be so worried.

I turned back to them and said, " How do we go back?"

Aisha said, " You need to draw that."

I looked at her in confusion, and said, " Draw what?"

Adnan said, " Maya, just like you drew this palace, you know how to get back as well. Your pencil will guide and rest we will do."

I felt bad that I would be leaving this place. He was nice though he was a ghost.

Jai said, " Maya, draw fast, please."

I looked at him and said, " Jai I don't know what to draw, please don't panic. It is a nice place here I am sure we can stay here till we find out a way."

He wasn't that convinced with my answer.

He said, " You don't want to leave?"

I looked at him and said, " What type of question is this?"

Adnan came in between and said, " Maya princess, here take this paper and here is your pencil. Take your time to find out the way."

He was about to go when I said, " Where are you going? Now you got her you forgot me completely?"

He looked at me confusingly and said, " What happened to you princess, how can I forget you?".

Chapter Eight

I was getting jealous, when Aisha said, " Why don't you both have this. It is very delicious."

We were thirsty , we drank it one go. It made us feel bit drowsy. They both had left. We were alone in the room. Jai was smiling and started laughing.

He came forward and said , " Maya, Maya, Maya, I love you so much. Promise me you will never leave me."

I got up and took few steps back and said, "I will."

He came behind me to catch. I was running , he catched my hands , and we fell on the bed. We were lost in each other's eyes. He slowly removed the hair which was falling on my face. He came bit forward and kissed me on my lips. He started by sucking my lower lips slowly taking my lips on his mouth. I could feel his tongue on mine, tongues were playing. We were smooching really hard. It turned to a deep long kiss. I pushed him away and walked towards the window.

He came behind me and held me by waist. He turned me towards him, and kissed me again. The kiss made us go towards the wall. He was wearing a shirt and jeans , I was wearing night gown. It had an over coat as it was sleeveless. He removed the knot of the overcoat. He kissed my shoulder, and he removed his shirt. He removed my gown by the sleeve. I was now just having my inners. His bare skin touched mine , I felt as if current passed by my whole body. He went on kissing my shoulder and neck. He slowly got hold of hook in my bra, he removed it as well. He removed his pants. He looked at my breasts and started pressing them and kissing them. He clasped my hands and slowly started sucking my breasts. My nipples were hard now. He removed my panties and his as well. He lifted me a bit higher in the wall and made my legs across his back. We were still kissing.

He put me down to the bed. He started kissing me all over so wildly and madly, I was moaning like crazy. He kissed my neck the most. He then came down to my breast again, he bit my nipple. He licked and kissed my belly. He went on kissing my inner thighs. He spread my legs wide , I was wet. He widened my pussy lips further, I knew he was going to lick. He licked it slowly first, in few moments he dug his tongue quite deep. His tongue was going up and down, he was licking real hard. I had got orgasm already. He got up and came towards me, he asked, " You sure of this?". I gave a shy smile which he understood was a yes. He first made my pussy long for his dick. He was playing around my pussy with his dick. Without any warning, he inserted his hard dick on my pussy. I screamed with pain, something like " AHhhhhhhhhhhhhh!" I don't know why we screamed like that. He got more excited , he took it out and inserted it more. I moaned more. He widened my legs more and rubbed my pussy with his fingers. He inserted his dick now in one go. I moaned louder. He started moving, going in and out. It was slow in the beginning. Later he clasped my hands and increased his speed. I could feel his heart beats increasing more than mine. He was nervous as well I guess. He ejaculated on me, I could feel him completely on me. I also got orgasm. He brought his face near me and we kissed again.

We slept on each other's embrace. I felt good to be in his arms. I cuddled when I opened my eyes.

He was smiling and said, " I don't believe this, I lost my virginity. But I am glad that it is with you."

I just smiled I didn't know whether to tell him or not. I got up from the bed, covering myself in the blanket, I said, " We need to get back to work."

He nodded. I had to meet Adnan and Aisha. I got back in my old clothes.

I could hear their voices. I went near them , they were just sitting and talking. I said, " I am sorry to disturb, I need to ask something."

They looked at me worriedly , I said, " Yesterday me and Jai had made out and I don't want to hide that I had made out with you before. I don't know if it's right or wrong."

They just smiled, Aisha said, " He didn't make out with you , it was me ." I look at her confusingly and say, " You sure?"

She says, " Yes. You don't need to tell that as well because it wasn't you."

I felt relieved. I come back and take out my sketch book. Jai comes near me and says, "This place is really beautiful, were this?"

I smile and say, "This is lost palace, same like the one I drew."

He says, "Oh yeah I remember."

He says, "I will go out and all, is it fine?"

I say, "Just ask them and go, it is better."

He says, " Na, no need I will sit here ,looking at you."

I blush and say, " Let me draw now, we have to go back also right?"

He says, " I don't know, I feel like we can stay for some days and then return. It feels like we are in some dream world. But we have to go, I want to make out with you more."

I smile, I say, " Yeah that is true, but what if I don't have voice when we return?"

He winks and says, " I fell in love with you when you didn't have a voice. I love you not your voice, even if you have or don't it doesn't make any difference to me."

I start blushing, I say, " Now keep quiet, and let me focus." I try to think but I don't get anything. My mind was going blank. I was going blank. All I could remember was making out with him and later on with Jai. I was getting paranoid. I look outside that is when I get idea. I start drawing slowly again. I drew sketch, I knew the way was coming up. It took long time but finally I drew the way out.

I went and showed to Jai. He was happy that we got way out. We took this to where Aisha and Adnan were sitting. They discussed how to get in there. They didn't waste any other moment. I looked all over as if I was leaving my house. First we were made to go to some old woman. She gave us both something to apply on our forehead. She asked us to repeat what she was saying. We did that as well. We were asked to close our eyes. It felt again as if we were flying. We had reached back but we didn't know which place it is. Now this was another big problem.

Adnan said, " Princess, we had got you back, now you need to leave."

Jai said, " Where? This is somewhere else."

Aisha smiled and said, " You can find it out I guess."

I got angry on this, I said," You said you will get us back , where is this place?"

She put her shawl on us and said, " Close your eyes."

I guess they were just playing with us. We were flying again. We landed in front of hospital.

Aisha said, " We keep our promises, we were just joking. Now come this way."

We were all walking, I saw my sister sitting there she looked so pale. She was drinking coffee.

I wanted to go near to her when Jai held me back, he said "No point Maya, they will not see you."

I look back at him with teary eyes, when Adnan comes in and says, " I will miss you , I had such a good time with you, I will never forget you and how much you helped us."

Jai was getting irritated, he said, " What did you do with her so much that you will miss her, you guys are ghost, you just used us to get things done, now please leave."

Adnan came towards me , held my hands and said, " I want to make love with you one last time as you not as Aisha."

I looked at him and withdrew my hands from him, I went towards Jai and stood behind him, he asked, "What happened?"

I just shook my head. Aisha said, " Jai come with me, it is time for you to return back." Jai said, " We will both go together. If I am going , Maya is also coming with me."

Aisha said, " It can't be, don't worry nothing will happen. Common you trusted us till here, we won't harm you or her now."

Jai was convinced enough .

He looked at me and said, " I will meet you soon. Don't worry." He left with Aisha. I was alone with him again.

I said with folded hands, " Please don't do anything, if you spend more time with me I will fall in love with you. Don't do that, it can't happen."

CHAPTER NINE

Chapter Nine

He held my hands tightly and came looked into my eyes. I was so lost in his eyes. He came forward and started smooching me, I had closed my eyes by then. He started sucking my lower lip, and slowly started kissing me hard. I was so lost in the kiss, my hands were moving through his hair. I held him tight against me, as if I didn't want him to leave. I withdrew myself when I was falling short of breathes. I started blushing.

He held my hands and said, " When I was making out with you even I felt many times, I wish you were Aisha in reality and I was alive. If I was alive I would probably choose you and be with you. It's not that I don't love her or anything, you are good soul. You agreed to sacrifice something which no one does normally. I am happy for you that you got Jai. I know you will miss me, but it will be fine. I am sure Jai will keep you happy and make you forget this like a dream."

I had tears in my eyes. I saw my family standing , they all looked tired. I wondered if anyone would believe me and my story. They would say I am mad. I look at myself laying down in the bed, I was surrounded by doctors. They also don't know what had happened with me. I go near me, in the bed and slowly push in as they had advised us. In few moments there is huge rush. Doctors were coming in and going out. My parents and sister were looking eagerly. After few minutes, I had regained consciousness. They were holding my hands and smiling, everyone looked happy. I saw Adnan and Aisha from inside. They both smiled at me and waved good bye. They were all showering me with kisses and hugs. I wanted to know if I had voice now or not but I didn't know what to ask. I try to speak but nothing comes out.

I knew it was just when I was there, I tried again, I asked, " Can I have water please?" Everyone looked at me shocked. I did have voice even now. It didn't go. I can speak , I can scream.

My sister came near me again, she hugged me and said, " We can talk from now on, you can gossip with me. I never knew lighting was enough for this."

My mom gives her small slap on shoulder and says , " Anything Diya, I am so happy that I can hear my Maya's voice from now on. "

I was moved to room from ICU.

My mother said, " Look who has come here?"

I look it is Jai. My face brightens up. I give a shy smile. He smiles the same way.

My sister says, " What is it with both of you? Like old actors, eye language?" He laughs hearing this and nods his head.

My sister says again, " Jai, you know what she can talk now. Miracle has happened."

He looks at me and winks. He behaves as if he didn't know, he says, " Is it true Maya? Say something I want to know how your voice is."

I say, " Yes it is true. How are you feeling now?"

He behaved as if he was shocked to hear me, he said, " Oh my God, this is so good, now we can talk finally."

Everyone was so happy that I could speak. Jai was on wheelchair, his parents also came to my room. We are family friends so they all knew me from childhood.

His mother came near me and said, " Now after you get job and all , no , whenever you feel like to get married, do that and come to my house. I want you to be together always."

Jai was blushing, it felt as if he was girl.

My father said, " It is up to them , we are ready whenever it is. "

My sister said, " No , we will have it together."

I said, " Chill , there is time why do you want to rush on it." I was feeling hungry .

I saw pen near by my desk. It was again all decorated with so many stones.

I try to reach it, when my father says, " This is from Romania, and this pen has a history. It has been passed on to many people through centuries."

I look at closely and wonder what history does this have, will it also have lustful prince trapped in it or a beast trapped in it.

My sister snaps my thoughts and says, " Oh hello, no more silence allowed. I am feeling hungry , can we go and eat something."

They all leave, I was with Jai alone in the room. It felt so good to be with him again.

He said laughingly, " I am happy you still have voice, which means I get to hear those sexy moans when I am in you."

He gave me lustful look.

I said, " Yeah, you wait, see who will moan more now."

He comes near my bed and says, " someone is too confident.'

I nod and say, " I have real hands on experience."

He smiles and says, " That was one time with me right?"

I sigh and say , " Hmm"

Chapter Ten

He looks at me again and asks, " Is there anything you are hiding Maya?"

I say, " I don't know if I should tell you or not."

He looks at me and says nervously, " Actually Maya even I have to say something."

I say, " Okay, you say first then."

He says, " Promise you wouldn't feel bad or say anything?"

I say, " I won't, the same goes with me as well."

We both exchange our experiences. I never knew even he had gone through the same what I have gone through. In the end we both felt as if we were used and cheated.

I ask, " What would they get by doing this?"

He takes deep breath and says, " Fun, they had good time with us. We were so innocent that we got used by ghost. We don't even know if they are alive or dead."

I say, " They are dead obviously."

He says, " You know if she was alive I would probably be in love with her, she is amazing. I don't have words to explain."

I look at him , he says, " Don't look at me like that, you know what I meant right?"

I nod, I say, “ Even I feel the same. His eyes and voice. He was too good with me. I don’t know if any man would be so gentle with a woman.”

Jai was feeling jealous. He said, “ Oh, okay. I thought I am gentle.”

I say, “ Don’t mix, we said we won’t get on each other. You weren’t bad either, I will get more of it in the coming days I guess.”

He blushed hearing this, he said, “ Obviously, whole life is there to experiment. I will try everything with you. I will make you mad over me that you will forget that guy.”

I laugh at his innocence, I say, “ Same here, I want you to forget her as well.”

He says, “ I have an idea , why not make this famous. We could write on erotic stuff and make people go mad reading this, pornography will be forgotten after that.”

I laugh, I say, “ What would we tell people, that there is pen which will talk to you later on if you are good in drawing you will draw stuffs and meet crazy girl or guy who will show you all faces of lust and pleasure?”

He said, “ No, you behave so dumb at times. We can write comics or something. You draw and I will write. It will be big hit. People would really go crazy I am telling you.”

I nod, idea wasn’t bad. I say, “ You mean I will have to draw people having sex?”

He started laughing , he said, “ You can get ideas from magazines like play boy and all. I will bring it if you want to.”

I give him disgusted look , he said, “ Okay fine , but we can write about it still. They did make us go crazy with pleasure.’

I say, “ Yeah and in the end say good bye. Don’t forget they aren’t alive.”

He says, “ That is main part. We can write anything, we just need to mix up imagination and what happened actually with us and make up the rest. You are good with pen and pencil. You can do it, the rest marketing and all I will do.”

I take a sigh and say , “ Okay, we will try.” He was happy that I agreed. Days went by, everything went back to normal. Everyone was excited and shocked to know that I can speak now. Jai and I became inseparable . Once we were fine, we had sex like crazy. In between I open my sketch book again. I thought of Jai’s idea. I write the first comic strip.

He reads it and smiles.

He says, “ You are genius. This is amazing. What shall we name this ?”

I look all around and say, “ Art trap.”

He says again, “ Art trap.”

Printed by Libri Plureos GmbH in Hamburg, Germany

9 798885 696791